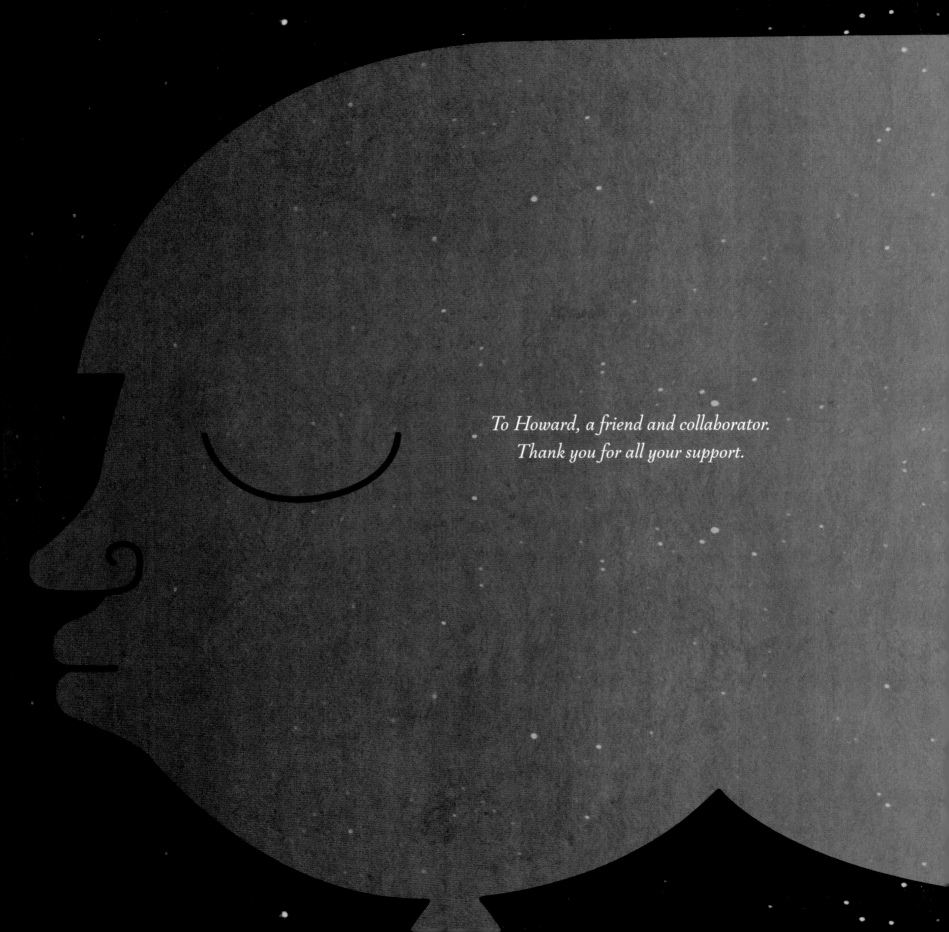

To Howard, a friend and collaborator.
Thank you for all your support.

A LAND OF BOOKS

DREAMS OF YOUNG MEXIHCAH WORD PAINTERS

DUNCAN TONATIUH

Abrams Books for Young Readers · New York

Our world, my brother, is an amoxtlalpan.*

In the jungles where the jaguar dwells, the Chontaltin make books. In the mountains, the Mixtecah, the cloud people, make them as well. So do others on the coast and in the forests. And we, the mighty Mexhicah who dwell in the valley of the volcanoes, make books too.

*A pronunciation guide and definitions for words in Nahuatl can be found in the back of this book.

Our parents are tlahcuilohqueh, painters of words. The amoxtin they make tell the stories of our gods, our history, our people. They work with others at the amoxcalli, the house of books. With the passing of time, their names will be lost like the smoke of incense when the wind blows. But their spirits shall remain. The words they paint will be sung by countless generations to come. One day, my brother, we will be painters of words too.

The amoxtin our parents make are long strips of paper with multiple page folds. On each end, they have covers made with wood. Our parents decorate the covers with the hides of jaguars, feathers, and precious stones. The books expand out. That is how the priests display them at the temple. They can also be folded down and stored easily at the amoxcalli.

Our parents make books with amatl, paper. I help them make it, and now you can too.

First we soak the bark of the amacuahuitl tree in water with limestone. We boil the mixture and smash it into a pulp.

We then press the pulp into thin sheets to dry.

Look at how colorful the amoxtin are! Our parents obtain the dyes to paint from plants, animals, and rocks. The most important paints are black and red. They are the sacred colors that tlahcuilohqueh use the most.

To make black paint we mix ashes with gum and water,

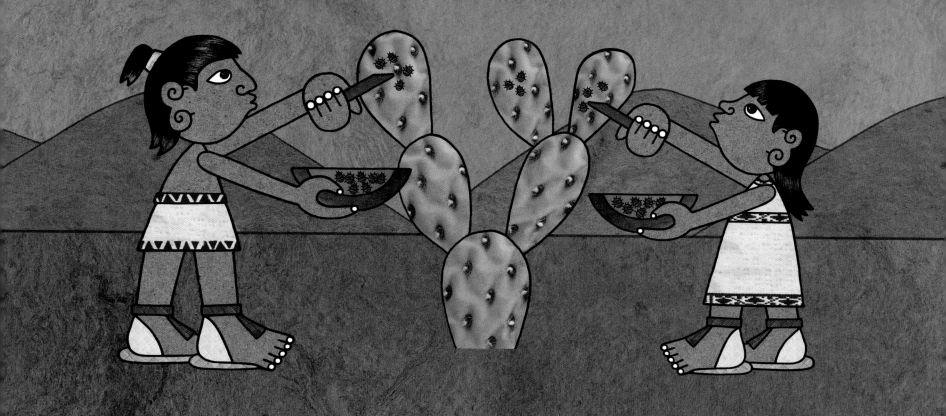

and to make red paint we collect the cochineal insects that live on the nohpalli.

We dry the bugs, crush them, and boil the red color they make with clay and water.

Father paints on amatl. But he also paints on walls when he decorates the temples, and he chisels words in stone when he carves images. Our grandparents taught him these arts, and in time, our parents will teach us.

But our parents also learned at the calmecac school. We will study there too. We will take classes alongside young nobles and warriors.

Father says a painter of words needs to know religion, astronomy, warfare, and history, among other subjects. Tlahcuilohqueh need to know a great deal to express knowledge with paint.

Not everyone can read the words our parents paint, though. Only noblemen, priests, and wise elders have access to the amoxtin and have been taught how to interpret them. They understand the colors and the layout of the pages.

They know why people sometimes look bigger than pyramids in the books. Those that cannot read the drawings may think they are strange. But everything in an amoxtli is painted as it is for a reason.

Tomorrow at the flower festival, the books our family has painted will be sung by a reader. That is when a macehualli, a villager, has a chance to hear the words and admire the images.

Tonight when we sleep, my brother, let us dream of amoxtin.

Let's dream of how, in the beginning, the universe was formless. But out of that darkness came the lord of what is near and far, who gave birth to four main gods: one in the north, one in the east, one in the south, and one in the west. He tasked these four Tezcatlipocah with the creation of the world and mankind.

Let's dream of the great migration.
Long ago our ancestors left Aztlan,
the island where they lived, after
the god Blue Hummingbird spoke
to them. He told them to search
for an eagle atop a prickly nohpalli.
After many years of pilgrimage, our
ancestors saw the sign and settled
on the shores of the Tetzcoco lake.
There, they flourished. They built
the great city of Tenochtitlan and
our powerful empire.

Let's dream about our great tlahtohqueh and how these leaders governed. The books show the enemies they defeated and who they wed to create alliances. Dream of amoxtin that are maps to define territories. And the books that track tributes—like shields, helmets, boxes of seeds, honey, and precious feathers—that the people we have conquered must send to our empire.

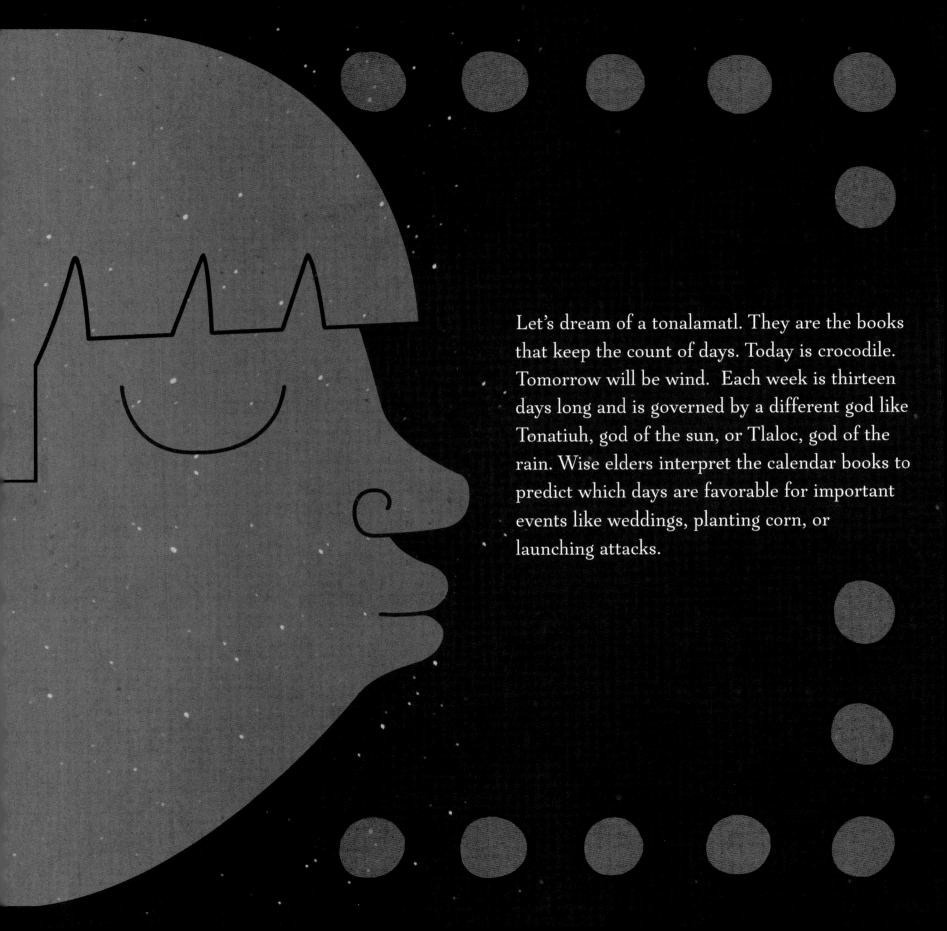

Let's dream of a tonalamatl. They are the books that keep the count of days. Today is crocodile. Tomorrow will be wind. Each week is thirteen days long and is governed by a different god like Tonatiuh, god of the sun, or Tlaloc, god of the rain. Wise elders interpret the calendar books to predict which days are favorable for important events like weddings, planting corn, or launching attacks.

And let's dream of the amoxtin about our sisters, the plants, and what illnesses they cure. Or about the movements of the moon and stars. Or of great battles and warriors. Dream now, my brother, of all the words, gods, people, animals, plants, and places we will one day paint.

Wake up, my brother! The day is here! We will soon leave for the plaza to attend the flower festival.

Look at the amoxtli! See the colors. Hear the performer sing the words our family painted. Listen to the drums, shells, and rattles play while the words are sung.

Watch the warriors dance as the amoxtli is read. Smell the smoke of
the aromatic copalli as it blows in the wind.

May our world always be an amoxtlalpan—a land of books!

GLOSSARY

I use the Nahuatl spelling and pronunciation for non-English words in this story, since the narrator is a Nahuatl speaker. In the Author's Note, I use the forms of the words that are commonly used in English (such as Mexica). Several Mesoamerican cultures spoke Nahuatl, and some Indigenous groups still speak it today. Many words of Nahuatl origin have become part of the Spanish language.

amacuahuitl: (ah-mah-KWAH-weetl) a type of ficus tree.

amatl: (AH-matl) paper that is usually made with the bark of a ficus tree. The use of amatl was so widespread before the Spanish arrived that it was one of the tributes that subjugated groups would send the Mexica empire. Amatl, or **amate** (ah-MAH-teh) paper as it is called in Spanish, is still made by artisans today.

amoxcalli: (ah-moash-KAL-lee) a house of books (singular).

amoxtin: (ah-MOASH-teen) books (plural). The Mexica and the Maya made books with paper made from plant fibers. The Mixtecs made books by covering the hides of deers with a thin layer of gesso that they could paint on.

amoxtlalpan: (ah-moash-TLAL-pan) a land of books; from the words amoxtli ("book") and tlalpan ("land").

amoxtli: (ah-MOASH-tlee) a book (singular).

Aztlan: (AS-tlan) an island where the Mexica claimed to have departed from before they arrived to the central valley region. The name Aztec is derived from the word **Aztecatl** (as-TEH-katl), which means "a person from Aztlan." Researchers are uncertain of where the island is. Some believe it is a mythic place and not a physical location.

Blue Hummingbird: refers to the god **Huitzilopochtli** (weet-see-loh-POACH-tlee), the god of war, and one of the most important deities for the Mexica.

calmecac: (kal-MEH-kak) a school where the Mexica nobility and warriors studied.

Chontaltin: (chon-TAL-teen) a Maya nation. The Mexica did not have a word for all Maya people. They referred to each separate Maya nation by a different name. The group they knew the best were the Chontal. The term *Maya* refers to a Mesoamerican civilization that existed for thousands of years and created some of the oldest pre-Columbian books that survive today. There are modern-day Maya in parts of Mexico, Central America, and the U.S.

copalli: (koh-PAL-lee) a resin from trees that can be burned to produce an aromatic smoke.

macehualli: (mah-seh-WAL-lee) a person in Mexica society that is not a part of the nobility or who doesn't hold high status. It typically refers to farmers and other workers.

Mexihcah: (meh-SHEE-kah) a Mesoamerican civilization that flourished between the fourteenth and sixteenth centuries. They were the most powerful civilization in Mesoamerica when the Spanish arrived to the region in the 1500s. In English, we usually refer to them as Mexica or Aztecs.

Mixtecah: (meesh-TEH-kah) a Mesoamerican group responsible for making some of the few pre-Columbian books that survive today. The Mixtecs, as we call them in English, called themselves Ñuu Dzahui, which means rain people or cloud people. There are modern-day Mixtecs in parts of Mexico and in the U.S.

nohpalli: (noh-PAHL-lee) a type of cactus.

Tenochtitlan: (teh-noch-TEE-tlan) the capital city of the Mexica empire. When the Spanish arrived, the city was more than five square miles and had an estimated 300,000 inhabitants.

Tetzcoco: (tets-KOH-koh) a lake in the central valley of Mexico. On the eastern bank of the lake, the city-state of Tetzcoco flourished. The Tetzcocans, or Acolhuas as they called themselves, were part of an alliance with the Mexica. The modern-day city Texcoco is located where the Mesoamerican city-state once stood.

Tezcatlipocah: (tes-kah-tlee-POH-kah) the four principal gods in Mexica mythology. They are associated with the creation of the world and humankind.

tlahcuilohqueh: (tlah-kwee-LOH-keh) plural of **tlahcuiloh** (tlah-KWEE-loh) which can be translated as scribe, painter of words, or painter of books.

Tlahtohqueh: (tlah-TOH-keh) the plural form of **tlatoani** (tlah-toh-AH-nee), which means governor or ruler.

Tlaloc: (TLAH-lock) the god of rain.

tonalamatl: (toh-nah-LAH-matl) a calendar book used for divination. The Mexica and other Mesoamerican cultures used two main calendars. One was a solar calendar that lasted 365 days, similar to the Gregorian calendar, which is the most widely-used calendar today. The other was a ritual calendar that tracked 260 days. There were twenty different symbols for the days. Some of them were crocodile, wind, house, lizard, and snake. Each week of the ritual calendar lasted thirteen days and each week was governed by a different god.

Tonatiuh: (toh-nah-TEE-w) the sun or god of the sun. Nowadays, it is sometimes used as a proper name. In English and Spanish, it is pronounced toh-nah-tee-YOU.

Thank you to David Bowles, an author, translator, and professor at the University of Texas Río Grande Valley for his help with the pronunciation guide and for sharing with me his expertise of the Nahuatl language.

AUTHOR'S NOTE

For thousands of years, before the Spanish and other Europeans came to the Américas, different civilizations flourished and disappeared in Mesoamerica, an area that extended from what is now the central region of Mexico in the north to Costa Rica in the south. Mesoamerican people had their own languages and beliefs. They built cities and pyramids. They made books too. In fact, Mesoamerica was one of the few places in the world where books originated and flourished without outside influence. The region was considered by its people as an amoxtlalpan, which means "a land of books" in Nahuatl.

Sadly, of the thousands—perhaps hundreds of thousands—of books that were made in Mesoamerica before the Spanish arrived in the 1500s, only fifteen survive. The Mexica (or Aztecs as we now refer to them) called books amoxtin, the Maya called them huun, and the Mixtecs called them tonindeye. Today we call the books they created codices.

The Mexica called the artists that painted books tlahcuilohqueh. They were both men and women, and highly respected. In pre-Columbian times, tlahcuilohqueh did not sign their work and it is believed that often more than one tlahcuiloh worked on a book.

Mesoamerican codices do not have written words in them, only drawings, but they can be read. The people in the codices are always drawn flat and facing sideways. Sometimes a person looks as big as a pyramid or a mountain. This is because the drawings in the books were not meant to be realistic. The drawings are stylized because they are pictograms. They are similar to and can be read like the emojis we use today. A reader could interpret the colors in the drawings, the positions of hands, and other elements to know the ranks and names of people depicted in the codices. A reader could also know the dates and the places represented, and understand the stories that the books told.

Mesoamerican codices were about a variety of subjects. Some were calendars. Others depicted the movements of the moon, planets, and stars. Some were about the gods and others about historical figures and events. Mesoamerican codices were probably about many other topics too. Perhaps some of them were books for children. Unfortunately, we will never know, as so very few are left.

When the Spanish conquistadores arrived in Mesoamerica to search for gold, they fought against the Mexica to take their land and resources. They were joined by the Tlaxcalans and other Indigenous groups that opposed the Mexica empire. During the 1521 siege of Tenochtitlán, the invaders, led by Hernán Cortés, set the capital city on fire. They destroyed temples and libraries where many codices were kept.

Many more codices were destroyed in the years following the Spanish conquest when Catholic priests began to arrive in the Américas from Europe. The clergymen wanted to convert the Indigenous people to their Christian religion. When they encountered Mesoamerican books, many priests thought that the books were the work of the devil. During the sixteenth century, clergymen searched for codices and burned them because they did not adhere to their religious beliefs.

It is impossible to know exactly how many Mesoamerican books were destroyed, but it was a large number. The bishop Diego de Landa wrote in the 1560s that he burned thousands of Maya documents and artifacts in a single day. The knowledge and stories that people of Mesoamerica had painted in books and collected over centuries were destroyed by the flames of a fire in a few hours.

Codex Fejérváry Mayer, detail. (See next page for more information.)

While almost all the codices that were made before the Spanish arrival were destroyed, there were many codices that were created soon after the conquest. These codices display a mixture of Meso-american and European traditions. They sometimes include words in Spanish, Nahuatl, or Latin. Some are made using amatl paper, but others are made with European paper. Instead of long strips, some are bound so that two pages face each other, the way most books do today. Many of these documents are maps and family trees that the Indigenous people made to show their new Spanish rulers why a piece of land belonged to them. About a hundred codices from that early colonial period survive.

But as the years passed, the creation of codices faded and Mesoamerican bookmaking traditions were almost fully replaced by European conventions and techniques. And sadly, many of the codices were taken from the land where they were made. Of the surviving pre-Columbian codices, only two of them remain in Mexico. The others are now in Europe. And while many early colonial codices are in Mexico still, many are in collections in Europe and the United States.

It is challenging for scholars to know how exactly the pre-Columbian codices ended up in Europe. Some were sent there soon after the conquest. From a letter Hernán Cortés wrote, we know that he sent two Maya codices along with other objects he had obtained in Mesoamerica to Carlos V, the king of Spain. Years later, the books were sold and bought, then resold by collectors. Some researchers believe that the books were lost, but others believe that one of the codices Cortés sent is the one that is currently at the Saxon State Library in Dresden, Germany.

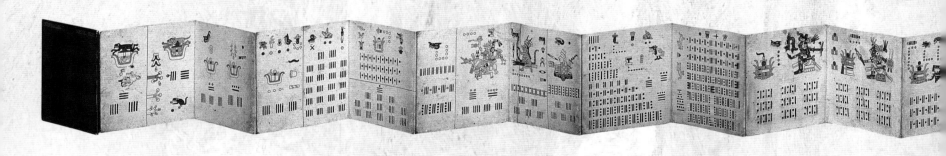

Other codices left the Américas hundreds of years later. Many were taken during the chaotic period after Mexico became independent from Spain in the 1800s. While different groups were busy fighting for power, the libraries and national archives were neglected. Thieves took advantage of this and stole some of the codices that were housed there. They sold them to foreign private collectors who had become interested in Mesoamerican art. Indigenous people who still owned some codices, and who often were struggling financially, sold them to private collectors too.

During the twentieth century, there was robust interest from the Mexican government to preserve Mesoamerican objects and art. In 1939, the National Institute of Anthropology and History was established. That is where the Mixtec Colombino Codex and the Maya Codex of Mexico are now kept. It is also where many early colonial codices are safeguarded.

Mesoamerican codices are extremely fragile because they were made with natural materials. They must be kept in special vaults at a specific temperature so that light and the elements do not deteriorate them. Very few people are allowed to handle them.

Fortunately, because of today's technology, we now have more access. Over the years, hand-painted reproductions of the codices have been made. The books have also been photographed and scanned. And now those reproductions are easily available online. Museums and organizations like the World Digital Library showcase them on their websites. The availability of these reproductions has renewed interest in the codices from researchers. We are still discovering new things about these ancient books, such as how to read the stories they tell.

Codex Fejérváry Mayer, unfolded, date unknown but before 1521. It measures approximately 160 inches (406.4 cm) wide x 7 inches (17.78 cm) high. When folded, it is approximately 7 x 7 inches (17.78 x 17.78 cm). The codex is named after two collectors that owned it. It is also known as the Tonalamatl of the Pochetecas—the Merchant's Book of the Days, or the Merchant's Almanac.

BIBLIOGRAPHY

Aguilar-Moreno, Manuel. *Handbook to Life in the Aztec World*. New York: Oxford University Press, 2007.

Aztec Books and Writing. See www.mexicolore.co.uk/aztecs/writing.

de Orellana, Margarita. *Codices Prehispánicos*. Mexico City: Artes de México, 2013.

Díaz, Gisele, and Alan Rodgers. *The Codex Borgia: A Full-Color Restoration of the Ancient Mexican Manuscript*. Mineola, New York: Dover Publications, Inc., 1993.

Dupey García, Élodie. "El color en los códices prehispánicos del México Central: identificación material, cualidad plástica y valor estético," *Revista Española de Antropología Americana* 45, no. 1 (2015). See revistas.ucm.es/index.php/REAA/article/view/52359.

Escalona, Enrique. *Tlacuilo*. Mexico City: CIESAS, 1987.

Galarza, Joaquín, and Krystyna M. Libura. *Para leer La Tira de la Peregrinación*. Mexico City: Ediciones Tecolote, 1999.

Gomez Sanchez, Sofia. "Materiales, formas y colores de los códices prehispánicos." August 15, 2016. See masdemx.com/2016/08/materiales-formas-y-colores-de-los-codices-prehispanicos.

González Morales, Leonardo Abraham. "The Tlacuilos and the Construction of the Novohis-Panic Space in the XVI Century." April 1, 2015. See revista.unam.mx/vol.16/num4/art29/art29.pdf.

Hessler, John. "The Codex Quetzalecatzin comes to the Library of Congress." November 21, 2017. See blogs.loc.gov/maps/2017/11/the-codex-quetzelecatzin.

León-Portilla, Miguel. "Códices. Los antiguos libros del nuevo mundo," *Anales del Instituto de Investigaciones Estéticas* 45, no. 81 (2002). See scielo.org.mx/scielo.php?script=sci_arttet&pid=S0185-1276200200200008.

Noguez, Xavier. *Códices*. Mexico City: Secretaría de Cultura, 2017.

Pardo López, José Manuel, José Antonio Peralbo Pintado, and Sergio Daniel Torres Jara. "Los códices Mesoamericanos prehispánicos." 2002. See ebuah.uah.es/dspace/bitstream/handle/10017/7585/codices_pardo_SIGNO_2002.pdf.

Siemens, Sandra. *Mi papá es un tlacuilo*. Mexico City: Norma, 2014.

Woodward, Hayley. "Painting Aztec History." See khanacademy.org/humanities/art-americas/early-cultures/aztec-mexica/a/painting-aztec-history.

WEBSITES WHERE YOU CAN SEE
REPRODUCTIONS OF CODICES

wdl.org

britishmuseum.org/collection

digital.bodleian.ox.ac.uk/collections/mesoamerican

guides.library.unlv.edu/codex

codicemendoza.inah.gob.mx

codices.inah.gob.mx (Spanish)

liverpoolmuseums.org.uk/artifact/codex-fejervary-mayer

amoxcalli.org.mx/codices.php (Spanish)

The images in this book were hand-drawn and then collaged digitally.

Cataloging-in-Publication Data has been applied for and may be obtained from the Library of Congress.

ISBN 978-1-4197-4942-1

Text and illustrations © 2022 Duncan Tonatiuh
Edited by Howard W. Reeves
Book design by Heather Kelly

Printed and bound in China
10 9 8 7 6 5 4 3 2 1

Abrams Books for Young Readers are available at special discounts when purchased in quantity for premiums
and promotions as well as fundraising or educational use. Special editions can also be created to specification.
For details, contact specialsales@abramsbooks.com or the address below.

ABRAMS The Art of Books
195 Broadway, New York, NY 10007
abramsbooks.com

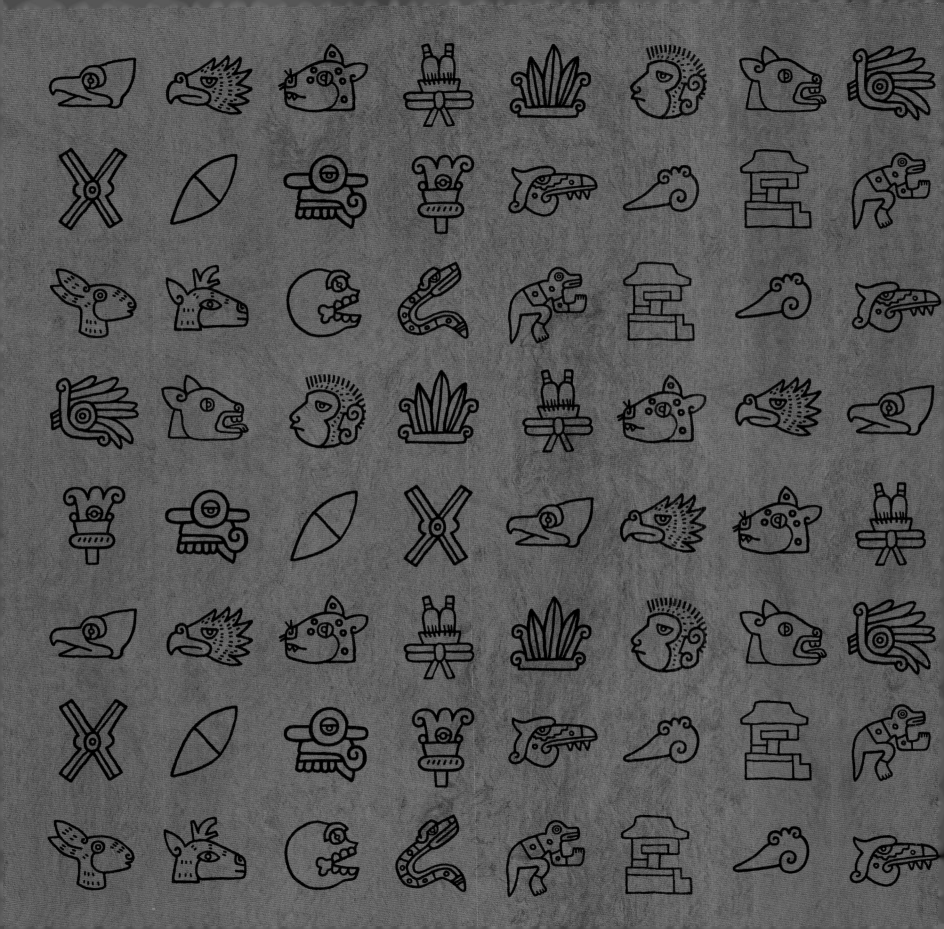